Percy
AND THE KITE

by Christopher Awdry
illustrated by Ken Stott

Lots of children were on their way to the grand kite-flying competition. "I want to fly a kite," said Percy dreamily.

"Engines don't fly kites," said Thomas. He remembered what had happened when he went fishing.
Percy scuttled off to take some trucks to the woodyard.

The foreman checked in the delivery.
"I'd love to fly a kite," said Percy, still dreaming.

"My son, Jake, is flying a kite in the competition," said the foreman. "You watch for it – it's a special green one."

The weather that day was bright and sunny with a strong wind, just right for flying kites.

As Percy steamed to the harbour, the kites were racing into the sky. Soon he spotted a big green one.

"That green one is flying well," said Percy's Driver.
As they drew nearer, Percy thought he recognised it.
He was right – it was a green engine just like him.

"That must be Jake's kite," said his driver.
Percy was thrilled. "Peep, peep, it's me – I'm flying,"
he whistled happily.

On their return journey the wind dropped. The kites began to dip and dive towards the ground. One even fell into the lake.

"What will happen now?" asked Percy anxiously.
"When the wind blows again it will soon carry them up,"
said his driver.

At the next station they met Thomas.
"Feeling hungry, Percy?" he called.

Percy was puzzled. "What does he mean?" he asked.
"I haven't a clue," replied his driver.

Toby was waiting at the top station.
"When does the party start, Percy?" he asked.

Percy's driver jumped down from the cab. He looked
at Percy's funnel and burst out laughing.

"Well, well, Percy," he exclaimed. "You've been flying a kite without knowing it." He unwound a string from Percy's funnel and showed him a kite like an iced cake.

Percy laughed. "So that's what you meant by a party, Toby," he said. "I wish we could really eat that cake."

They took the cake kite back to the field on their next journey. They arrived just in time to see the First Prize being given to ...

... Jake, for his kite shaped like Percy.
"I won, I won," whistled Percy excitedly. "That's even better than flying a kite."

Well done, Percy and Jake.